REGICIDE
ON THE
51st FLOOR

An Aversion Bureau novel.

S.R. Ringuette

SRR Publishing

First Edition

ISBN: 0987941429
ISBN-13: 978-0987941428

This book, and the many still to come, are dedicated to Annette and David Ringuette who taught me how to tell stories and how to make them funny.

Also for providing the basic genetic material prerequisite to my existence, were I capable of doing that on my own, this would be a very different book.

The first Aversion Bureau novel!

The Aversion Bureau was a webcomic that updated absurdly frequently from 2011 to 2013 at a website of the same name.

But you don't need to know what any of that means in order to enjoy this story. The comic has ended but the world lives on, in this, the first Aversion Bureau novel:

Regicide On The 51st Floor.

—— CONTENTS ——

Beautiful and simple like a dumb, sexy triangle

Agent Max Martin of
The Aversion Bureau awoke to
the sight of his reflection in the
pavement and immediately knew
that something was wrong.

PHASE ONE

I don't remember putting gel in this morning, was the first thought that came stumbling through Max Martin's mind as consciousness made itself known once again. He reached up to the certifiable bouffant of a hairdo his hands expected to find, as they had done so many times before, only to have them return bright red. *So clumsy,* he thought, *raspberries are not a hand fruit after all.*

"Agent, stand up." A voice accosted him.

"Wipe that blood from your eyes and *stand up.*"

Blood? Reality was returning to Max more suddenly than could be considered polite. Propping himself up on wobbling wrists, the once-handsome concrete mirror now revealed itself to be a small pool of blood. Probably his, but really, who knew? Looking around, the parking lot clarified and those green blurs in the distance took the forms of trees. The white blurs, however, remained blurry. *Clouds,* he posited.

Standing above Max was a short, lean, formidable woman with tied-back blonde hair and a stern expression set around condescending green eyes. "Beautiful, but in a way that inspires fear," he accidentally narrated aloud. The woman ignored it with naught but an eyebrow twitch to acknowledge the faux pas.

"Agent Martin we are faced with a problem," the woman informed as he climbed to his feet.

"What? I mean, somebody bled all over the ground, yes, but . . . what kind of problem?"

"A matter of extremely localized hubris," she insisted, tone unchanged. He squinted at her.

Max could never tell when Agent Stone was trying to be funny. Even when she said things that one would assume were meant as humour, her gaze would still unsettle his stomach. It was ironic, he often thought, that her surname would be Stone given how well it matched her personality. *It must be a coincidence, because if people were given last names AFTER their birth based on their behaviours most of us wouldn't be able to make it to a year old without being called Dribbleshits.*

"Are you with me, Agent Martin?" Stone regained his attention loudly.

"Only as much as ever, tell me what we're doing next," Max replied, standing dizzily now.

"The first step is to get back inside the building . . . the last step, is to kill our boss."

That was when Max noticed that she was bleeding too.

Max Martin and Agent Stone were of a height at roughly five-foot nine, although if you were measuring with hair included he would have a sudden and considerable advantage. Max was fair-skinned, smooth-faced, brown-eyed and thin. He wore a virginal white button-up shirt with a bright red tie and black pants a *little* too short in the leg. The kind of ensemble you wear to work in an office building when you've never done so before. The only remarkable feature about this twenty-something man was his outrageous hairdo. A mix of Elvis and catastrophic negligence created a towering black sea-cliff that could not be tamed. Despite all of this, in that moment, Max felt like a proper man. He reached to inspect his colleague's arm wound imbued with all the medical knowledge eight seasons of *House* could provide.

"I am bleeding but I am not *hurt*," She snapped, recoiling from his touch. "I will bandage up your forehead before we go any further though, you're likely to freak out if you see the wound you received last night."

Max smiled internally. *I bet it was heroic, whatever I did.* Agent Stone revealed a bandage from her jet-black jacket and began to dress his wound while they stood in the parking lot, surrounded by yards of green grass and beyond that, a deep forest of tall pine trees. Initially Max recoiled at what he thought was a feminine hygiene product but quickly realized he was just being silly.

Now entirely aware of his surroundings and in full control of his faculties, Max glanced sidelong towards his place of work: 'RGI insurance'. It was a colossal steel and concrete office building consisting of fifty-one total floors with a whole bunch of radar antennas and crap on top. In truth though, he worked for no mere insurance company. Only the first twenty floors of this building were designated for the company 'Really Good Insurance', the purveyors of any and all things that could be classified as insurance. For clarification on what that might entail, Max would probably have to actually talk to somebody who worked there sometime. The next thirty floors of the building placed above the toil of the common man, were windowless. Thirty windowless floors hiding the greatest misdirection of all, *The Aversion Bureau*, a top-secret hideout for the world's most dedicated and yet woefully-mismanaged apocalypse prevention agency. An agency that attempts to thwart the unimaginable evils of the world on a budget. These thirty extremely conspicuous additional floors were initially explained as *Japanese luck floors*, a high-concept architectural ideal from the Far East. Quite luckily, nobody had questioned it since. Perched atop this institution of deceit and coverage-despite-low-credit-scores was the *fifty-first floor*. That floor *had* windows and over-compensatingly large ones to boot; that floor was the office of Director Thomas Bilge, the eccentric founder and leader of The Aversion Bureau. It was that final floor that held all the answers.

Stone gave Max a tap on the shoulder when she was done and beckoned towards the front door of the building, a large glass double entrance that seemed to say "Come on in," whilst the large black text someone had scrawled from the inside-facing-out literally read "ORGY – NINTH FLOOR", which struck him as odd. As the pair walked the wide, cracked-concrete path to the entrance of the building, Agent Martin looked back towards the lot and noticed how many cars were still parked there. This was strange, because his memories were now suggesting that today was Saturday, a day when no one except the agents of the Aversion Bureau could be expected to show up. *Who do these cars belong to?*

"Last night our fearless leader, Director Bilge, threw a massive office party for the civilians downstairs, saying that it was for the wonderful accomplishment of selling '*a great deal*' of insurance this quarter. . ." Agent Stone began explaining, her tone changing to one of shame as she continued. "Now it becomes increasingly clear that this was likely a cover so that he could raid the secret liquor stores whilst keeping me distracted. Everything fell to pieces from there. You know how Bilge gets when he's had too much to drink."

Max nodded grimly, remembering an incident two years ago during an office Halloween party where a fellow agent was thrown straight through a wall for daring to insult the director's honour by laughing at his costume. The incident eventually resolved in a massive room filled with bean-bag chairs, a fittingly strange end to a night that defied reason. When allowed too much to drink, an unpredictable, primordial aristocrat awakens in Director Bilge - an avatar of insanity and Victorian-sensibility that guarantees destruction wherever it goes, regardless of his intentions. But the director was by no stretch of the imagination an evil man, far from it, and so how this party ended in bloodshed and their exile to the parking lot, Max still had no idea.

"But you're Bilge's favourite! You're his right hand man-slash-*lady*, and you *never* let him out of your sight when drinks are involved. How did he manage all that?" He questioned her as they swung the large glass double-doors open to enter the RGI Insurance ground floor lobby. She looked at him briefly, then clearly deigned not to answer and picked up her pace towards the receptionist's desk. *She never trusts me with anything. I can't become a better agent if I'm always expected to play the bumbling sidekick. When will I finally get the chance to become a bumbling leader?* Max stewed as he looked around for any indication of exactly *how* everything went wrong at this party, finding evidence enough to set a *CSI* team to work for a decade. The lobby area of the insurance company was a sensibly-styled modern disaster zone. Stylish waiting area sectionals had become the ramparts and battlements of many an abandoned fortress, empty bottles of hard liquor littered the tiled marble floor and the gross misuse of post-it notes was astounding. As Max followed his cohort across the room, he noticed a small saucer on the receptionist's desk, with an empty bottle of bourbon resting on the rim. Some of the damage around him was as meticulous and nonsensical as any drunken fool could aspire to, with potted plants uprooted, inverted, and replaced throughout the lobby. If only Max had a before-and-after picture of this place, he could spot the differences until the red ink ran dry.

"There are people passed out in that conference room, I can see them through the glass. *And* I'm pretty sure I just stepped on a string of condom wrappers, which scared me because I thought it was a snake." Max scowled downwards at the condom-snake, shuddering. "Just how big *was* this office party?"

"Comically over-sized," Stone replied. Max chuckled, but was glared down.

She was doing that thing again.

At the rear of the lobby, beyond most of the

7

carnage, two elevators were set into the pristine off-white wall. One was as picturesque as any stainless steel elevator could be save for a few crude renderings of a penis belonging to someone from accounting, according to the inscription, at least. Max was not otherwise familiar with this particular penis. The other elevator was decidedly more run down and appeared at first glance to be out of order. At second glance however, one could see that "OUT OF ORDER" was in fact a recurring phrase on the yellow tape strung around it. This was the 'secret' elevator that agents of the Aversion Bureau would use to travel beyond the first twenty floors of the building, beyond the face of the company and deep into the heart of the building. Agent Stone swiped her identification card repeatedly into the reader that was set beside the door and was greeted by a series of increasingly defiant beeps.

"I believe that this malfunction is deliberate," Stone spoke over the incessant robotic chirping.

"Unless. . . your card is. . ?" Martin leaned in and inspected his partner's access card. The black magnetic strip was indeed facing the right direction, which was often a problem for him. "Well then, sabotage it is."

She spun to face him. Serious as death. "Agent Martin, right now our boss is up there, with an unlimited supply of quality alcohol, making decisions that could turn our agency from the force of good that it is into a circus of misspending and insanity that will affect the livelihood and safety of hundreds of innocent people. Do you recall when he traded our passes to the Global Defence Summit in Brussels for tickets to the opera?"

"Yes. . . but, you wouldn't go, so he took me with him. I got to dress up nice, and it was beautiful." Max allowed himself a moment of reminiscence.

Stone sighed and continued. "Last night when I realized how far the celebration had flown off the rails I went up to Bilge's office and demanded that he calm down and send everyone home. At this point he was already wearing a lampshade for a crown and using an antique saber to decapitate wine bottles. You were there, amongst others, being put to trial for the 'crime of sobriety'."

"I've never been so drunk that I couldn't remember anything. That can't be all."

"Shortly after my arrival Bilge and I came to blows. I stormed out of the building and you followed, insisting on the paramount importance of my protection," Stone continued.

That must be how I got this wicked head wound. . Max was momentarily lost again in the imagined bravery he unknowingly achieved last night.

"The sun is only just finished rising; these drunken office drones are on the verge of waking up. We must stop Bilge at all costs, before he runs the

Bureau into the ground." Her tone was unexpectedly sincere.

Max went to one knee and bowed his head, grinning at the thought of how cool he felt at this one particular moment. "For the Bureau," he spoke solemnly, as a knight might swear his sword.

"If you don't get in this elevator immediately, you're fired."

Max lifted his head and found Agent Stone standing in the working elevator to his left, brow furrowed and looking characteristically impatient. He scurried after her. The elevator door shut and lurched into vertical motion headed directly to the twentieth floor. This was the last floor of RGI Insurance, from which they could take the stairs to reach the hidden Bureau above since the proper elevator refused to help them. Max stood in stiff silence hoping to make no further fool of himself for at least the duration of the elevator ride.

"We're going to make our way to Agent Andersen's lab on floor thirty one. A safe haven from partying of any variety, and get him to reactivate the elevator. Then it's a straight line to the last floor and stopping Bilge."

"Will we need any more help?" Max asked, "I might still be drunk."

"If any other agents are still here, we'll find

them."

The elevator came to an expectedly stomach-churning halt at the twentieth floor and dinged excitedly as it opened. Stone leapt out, checked both directions and took off to the left in a brisk jog, her ponytail flowing behind her, her black running shoes padding softly on the carpeted floors. Agent Martin panted behind her, suddenly becoming aware of a pounding hangover that hid below the surface of his initial head trauma. He noticed that the depressingly patterned grey-carpeted hallways of the insurance company were considerably more drab than he expected. This revelation flying directly in the face of everything his parents tried to teach him about the magnificence of an office job entered after four years of a directionless college degree. As it turns out, small-time secret agent and world-saver was a better gig. Even on the days when you wake up to forgotten injuries and the news that you'll spend a day deposing your insane drunken boss. Nine times out of eleven, that beats a decent paycheque earned safely. Or so read his diary.

The hallway was long, unremarkable and littered with discarded bottles of brown and green glass. Red plastic cups and more than a reasonable amount of missing clothing populated the areas of the hallway around where the agents placed their feet before each step as well. There were multiple left hand turns before the stair access came into view, finally, at the end of a particularly messy bend of the hall. There was confetti on the ground here. Was this the site of a truly significant event last night, or perhaps a simple anomaly? Max occupied his thoughts imagining these scenarios while the ghosts of liquor's past rang gongs of disapproval with each pounding jog.

"In here!" Stone shouted back as she passed an open conference room and stopped to try and pull open the stairwell door at the end of the hall. But it was locked, and no amount of frantic jiggling would convince it to change.

Then as Max passed the same open door on his way to assist with the jiggling, something moving caught his eye, and he stumbled to a halt. Peering inside he found a mass of human flesh. At least a dozen inconsistently clothed, sleeping women were arranged haphazardly on and around a large conference table surrounded by expensive leather chairs. As far as he could tell all of these people were alive, which was in all honesty, a pretty big relief.

"Are any of you suffocating in there?" He felt the need to check before moving on.

"*Quiet! You'll wake the ladies!*" A voice whispered back, commanding but gentle.

Where the pile of sleeping women was deepest, right in the center of the table, there now stirred something beneath the surface. The silhouette of a very lucky man rose carefully from its depths, those women who were previously clinging to him now sloughed off like a leper's flesh and re-settled on the pile, remaining shockingly undisturbed. The man stepped from this pile, across the room and towards Max, quiet as an introverted shadow at a large social gathering. He grabbed Max by the collar of his shirt and lifted him out of the room as though he weighed nothing at all.

"Bro. What do you want? I was in my happy place." The man was none other than Dick Davison, senior agent of the Aversion Bureau and 'widely famed lover'. Self-proclaimed, but it was hard to argue with his results. His breath smelled of mixed liquors and testosterone.

Standing easily more than a foot taller than Max, Dick Davison was a bronze-skinned goliath of a man, perpetually clothed in a sleeveless yellow work-out shirt that made his already massive pectorals look positively *triangular*. Dick put Max back down on the ground and crouched down so that their faces were level. His smile was the sly mask of a man who had achieved something.

"Did you. . ?" Max began.

"Did I *what*? Did I bang out a *sex-symphony* with this orchestra of bodacious babes from the sales department last night? You *could* ask that. . . but a gentlemen never tells." Davison lovingly patted his friend on the head and looked down the hallway, throwing his hands up at Agent Stone. "Ladybro! What's

13

with the rushing around? You almost woke my sexpile."

The stern agent stood at the end of the hall with her hands behind her back, exasperation rippling under the surface of her otherwise cool demeanor. "Agent Davison, we are currently experiencing a code *white*." Dick sprung to attention at the mention of it and vaulted down the hall, smashing open the stairwell door effortlessly with his massive shoulder as Agent Stone quietly stepped aside.

He turned back to them. "Last time this happened, Bilge lost my Lamborghini in a bet with some demons from the friggin' gambling dimension. It's not even company property, bro!" Dick slammed one massive fist into the doorframe, denting it, and grimaced. "It's time for *plan two*."

"Step two," Agent Stone corrected.

". . . *Phase* two?" Max suggested quietly from down the hall with a small raise of his hand. The trio of agents shared a look for a moment and nodded in agreement.

Dick Davison gestured towards the door and the other agents ran up to follow him through. "This is why we keep you around, bro," said Dick, smiling.

"I thought it was for my witty one-liners." Max smirked back.

Their only response was footsteps.

REGICIDE ON THE 51st FLOOR

PHASE TWO

The three agents stood in front of a blank, knob-less door on a drab concrete landing that went no higher in this stairwell, just one short flight of stairs above where they had anticlimactically climbed from moments ago. They were now on the *twenty-first* floor. The first floor of the Aversion Bureau, the first floor of this towering building *hidden* to the public eye, and the first floor of what was certain to be a cavalcade of needlessly wacky obstacles.

Each of these three people were sworn and hardened agents of the Aversion Bureau. Agent Max Martin was the greenest having only been with them for a little over two years, Agent Dick Davison for over seven, and their superior, the deadly and diminutive Agent Stone had been with the Bureau since its founding. When the problem is supernatural, extra-terrestrial, or just plainly too *awesome* for the public consciousness, these brave folks were among the dozen or so agents that the Aversion Bureau had to offer. Some problems of global importance are handled by the FBI while others are handled by MI6 or organizations older and even further shrouded in mystery. The Aversion Bureau's reach was more localized than that, often working on leads that the men at the adult's table left behind as scraps. Despite this, each agent of the Bureau had won more honour and protected more lives than any normal person could reasonably hope for in a lifetime. But on *this* day, all of that was undermined by the task before them: dropping everything to stop their own founder from ruining his legacy.

And on *Saturday*, of all days.

Dick Davison traced the seam of the doorframe that sat before the group pensively, pretending to look for a way to open it without immediately jumping to his standby solution of muscles.

"Is this going to be a 'speak FRIEND and enter' kind of situation?" interrupted Max. "Because I've come across that a *surprising* amount of times in this line of work."

Agent Stone shook her head disapprovingly while she carefully unpinned the little badge perpetually pinned high on the left side of her chest. It was a small square crest with a 'T', an 'A' and a 'B' arranged into one design. This badge was the same as the ones given to any member of the Bureau, except that hers was decidedly less *made-in-China*. Stone felt around the dinted and dusty door until she found a set of grooves, impossibly small and invisible to anyone who wouldn't know where to look. Pressing her badge into the matching indents, the door clicked open in response, and with a gentle push the group was inside. All three agents stepped up and moved forward in unison. This hall was dim, scuffed, and likely unchanged since the building first went up. "Remember, with the elevator out, we're playing in a puzzle box. Each floor accesses the next in a different way, usually by ladders or stairs, but not always."

"There are two paths Ladybro, you go left and I'll take Max with me." Dick hurried them along.

Agent Stone nodded and took off left, down an identical stretch of hallway to the first and the next, lit with dim bulbs, lined with closed doors bearing the names of their contents: *brooms, buckets, mops, live bait, important hats and hats of lesser importance.* The usual. Max shortly realized he had been down to this floor before, sent to retrieve the director's favourite cricket bat, he had spent six hours locked in the wickery grip of a Chinese finger trap he had found instead. Those were simpler days.

Agent Davison piped up while they made their way down the wide hallway towards a turn at the end. "Man we're lucky that door we just got through wasn't one of the *Thursdoors*. I was worried it was going to be."

"*Thursdoors?*" Max repeated.

"Yeah bro, real pain in the ass, only open on Thursdays," Dick said matter-of-factly.

"That exists? We *have* those?" Desperate for an explanation, Max insisted.

"One for every Thursday of the month. If you're ever on the forty-second floor and need to piss on a Wednesday. . ." Dick Davison absently mindedly made a fist over his crotch, and slowly expanded his fingers outwards while peeking into an open doorway. "Lesson learned," he said remorsefully.

"*Two years* here and I somehow didn't realize I was working for God-damn *Willy Wonka*. . ." Agent Martin trailed off as he began to detect a faint buzzing sound coming from *somewhere*.

". . .Dude, a chocolate river would be sick right about now. . . *do you hear that?*"

BRAZZAP!

"*Jesus Christ - my nipples!*" Yelped the smaller agent, leaping backwards and covering his chest with his hands. In front of him hovered a small, oval shaped and heavily tarnished silver robot propelled by a single beanie-like propeller atop the center of its body. It had a little camera functioning as one cycloptic eye and a frail arm holding a lit taser out in front of itself in a mockery of menace. Buzzing determinedly and hovering in a loopy bell curve, it attempted to re-stabilize and mount another attack. Max looked over at his partner, the massive man Dick Davison, consumed by laughter and wiping tears from his eyes as he attempted not to re-live his tale of lost bladder control.

"That- *hah hah*- that's a security drone. From like, ten years ago! I'm amazed it works! Those things really shouldn't be activated bro, but at least it's too cute to harm anybody." Dick collected himself and thumped his partner on the back.

"Speak for yourself." Max spat as he slapped the tiny robot off-balance when it came back to peck again at his tender breast. It spun away, looking inebriated.

It was at this moment they both heard Agent Stone yell back to them from seemingly not far down the other path, she had found the way to the next floor. Max left the pitiful machine to its unsightly aerobatics and followed his friend.

"Bro, I can't *wait* to tell Stone how a robot zapped you in the tit." Davison began to laugh again but cut himself off. Max didn't have to wonder why for long as a deafening, droning torrent of buzzing noise flooded the air around them. Between where they stood and the direction Agent Stone had called from, dozens of robots, identical to the one from moments ago and in various states of disrepair, poured from the storage closets that lined the hallway and loped towards the agents. As pathetic as they seemed individually, this tide of steel that bore down on them now managed to achieve some measure of intimidation. Though Dick Davison did nothing but smile, rev his arms in a windmill and charged, giggling like a boy, into the press of metal. If the miniscule electric shocks bothered him, it was a secret that died messily. Agent Martin tried to keep up, staying within the wake of his colossal compatriot's clanking carnage. Davison's fists smashed metal and plastic, propeller and shell alike. Truly these robots were not worth what the agency paid for them, but despite their fragility it was disturbing to see that Director Bilge had actively taken steps against their progress.

Suddenly, Max took a shock in the ankle from behind and tripped forward, smashing his bandaged head against a mostly un-damaged drone that must have slipped through the wall of Dick ahead. He yelled out and hit the ground hard, sliding a few feet. With a slowly approaching cloud of the little bastards coming on, Max swung for the fences, left and right and left again, having little effect besides cutting his knuckles on propeller blades and burning his fingers on their tasers. He managed to stand back up and stumbled after his partner before they were completely on him. Obnoxious electric shocks burning his back as he swatted his way through the iron cloud. His march was hard-fought as the seconds ticked on, and he retained no dignity with the noises he made, but eventually the drones attacking him ceased their incessant electric stinging. *Probably ran out of battery.* Max relished the thought, yet they continued to bump and stumble into him like thirty buzzing steel puppies desperate for love, smothering him slowly into the floor. "Dick! *Help!* It's like I'm drowning in old people!"

A hand reached in, grabbed his wrist and yanked him safely out of harm's way. A softer hand than he expected. Then a shapely flurry of kicks rained over him followed by a hail of screws, bolts and lenses. The precision fury of Agent Stone's shoe-based arsenal swung high and low, bringing death to the final few clamouring machines. She pulled him to his feet and pointed towards the end of the hall. Agent Davison stood there under a string that dangled from the ceiling, and Max noticed there was a small, smiling cat key-chain tied to the end of it. Dick held it up to him, beaming stupidly and pulled hard. A stucco flap swung away from the ceiling and a heavy wooden ladder slid from the space it made, which to Max seemed like the closest replacement for an elevator they were going to get. Agent Stone caught up and addressed them while wiping small pieces of robot from her coat. "Not much of a deterrent, but the message was clear. Status?"

"Feeling strangely sad for the tiny robots," reported Max, surveying the damage listlessly. In truth he was quite hurt, his right nipple and lower back ached in the way that only getting tased sixteen times by tiny robots can inflict. Somehow though, it seemed to have cured his hangover. He would have to remember this.

"*SWEATY* and *EXCITED*," beamed Dick Davison whose chest rose and fell rapidly with frequent breaths. His shirt was scuffed and singed, his buzzed, dark brown hair flecked with oil. He was the first up the ladder with Stone following and Max taking up the rear. When Agent Martin looked straight up the ladder shaft, it seemed to go higher than just one floor upwards, but mostly he just saw asses. The trio padded along up the ladder in silence until they reached the top, emerging through a slab of false tile in a small and dusty broom closet on some floor well above where they started. They sat down on the floor, catching their collective breath, when suddenly Max's phone started going off in his pocket. Some kind of notification. He took it out and read, his expression changing from confusion to worry, skipping recognition entirely. "Alright, you two might be interested in something I've just found for sale in the classifieds. . ."

"*Extremely unlikely.*" Stone began to speak but Max raised his palm at her and continued.

"Someone under the name *TommyB* is offering a 'whole load of sciencey bollocks' for sale in our area. Some of this stuff looks pretty high-tech. Apparently he's also willing to trade for the equipment's value in gold bullion, or sapphires. *Specifically* sapphires. Do you think that's Bilge?"

"That's probably him. Why he needs *more* money, I have no idea, but we can't afford to lose that lab equipment. We'll have to quicken our climb." Stone

23

finished on the same breath she started, visibly impatient. "MORE Importantly, I think, *bro*, is that you get notifications on your phone from classifieds? *Why?*" Dick interjected.

"I. . . I read a lot of personals, and I only get notified for listings close by." Max cleared this throat and packed away his phone, breaking eye contact with his colleague. "*Besides.* . . sexy singles are sometimes in my area, and, *you know.* . . I like a heads-up." As they all rose to get moving again, Dick gave him a pitiful smile and the most awkward knock-on-the-arm that any of them had ever seen, before opening the door to leave the tiny white broom closet and find out how high the ladder had taken them.

The massive space greeted the agents with warm, soft lighting and the faint smell of fabric freshener. It looked to be nearly as wide and long as the building itself, as though the entire floor was one large room. Somehow, it still possessed a dream-like quality. Max could see nothing populating the room besides a surprisingly large amount of colourful fabric chairs, huge speakers set into each of the four corners and a single door in the opposite wall next to the currently useless elevator. Stone, Davison and Max made their walk briskly across the room towards the door, footsteps echoing on the tiled floor in the abundance of empty air. About a quarter of the way through it became clear that the chairs were arranged in two immense circles, red and blue, that overlapped in the center of the room, creating a smaller oval where they were coloured purple-grey. Agent Martin had never seen this floor before but decided not to be a bother by asking his cohorts to explain yet another aspect of the job to him. There were many times a day, working for the Aversion Bureau, where he would find himself flabbergasted at what he was being asked to do, and where it was supposed to occur.

They must think him some kind of idiot, but did they even understand how much he cared about this job? Nothing in his life has been so important to him, he had finally found a purpose, something noble like he always imagined he could have when he would read adventure stories as a kid. *Now,* he hadn't finished a book in years, but epic as was the job of a secret agent, he put up with plenty of insanity just to fit in here. So *what* if It took him a while to learn how to fire a gun without peeing a little, and the first time he went up against the wrestle-bot back in training he broke a load-bearing pillar with his own face? *Jesus. . .* he WAS pathetic, it's not like he'd gotten much stronger since then. . . and the job didn't get any less strange, why did they even keep him around? Dick is a mountain and Stone was probably a professional assassin before she got here, what do I *have?* Well what I *haven't* had is a girlfriend, in five years, that's what. I read "The Game" and watched all the Youtube videos, but still no luck. Can't even look Agent Stone in the eyes, they're so green. So powerful, it makes me shrivel up. I am NOT breeding stock, and was probably lucky to get the freaking gas-station job I had *before* the Bureau. The closest thing to a friend of mine who isn't on a digital list is Dick and standing next to him makes me look like a cardboard cutout made entirely of factory errors . On top of all that, I'm a shitty artist and not good enough at video games to move to Korea to get famous. . . *Oh my God my mother even forgot to invite me for Christmas dinner last year-*

MAX!

Agent Martin whipped back to reality to the stimulus of a huge hand messing up his hair. "Oh man, it got you good! Snap out of it bro!" Max looked around to find he had taken a seat, on one of the blue chairs that came before the overlapping oval in the centre of the room. Judging from the direction of their entrance he had just walked through the wide ring of blue chairs and come to this one, though he had no recollection of when he had stopped walking or *why*. Dick Davison was standing over him, chuckling and Agent Stone was almost at the other end of the room, ignoring them both.

"What the *hell?*" Max mustered, blinking repeatedly to validate the notion that this was in fact the real world he was now seeing.

Dick pulled him to his feet by his thin red tie, always smiling, and began to walk again. "Bro, this is *The Room Of Introspection.* Big ol' chair circles and a tone playing through the speaker that does a bunch of science on your brain and makes you think about your life and your feelings and stuff. Stone and me, we've been here before, you get used to it and learn how to fight it. Forgot you were just a big newbie though," he winked.

Max continued to walk in silence, for what seemed a long time, frowning as he attempted to catch the fleeting thoughts left in his mind after what could only be described as a gross manipulation of his mental state. If he could find the floor with the office psychologist, he'd be making a stop there after today. The pair kept walking between the rows of colourful chairs, catching up to their third member. But most of the way across the room, lost in thought, it took Max a good few steps to realize that Dick was in fact *not* beside him. He turned and found him *way* back, crouched down and balancing on the balls of his feet, running thick fingers over a furrowed brow.

". . .Dick?" Max addressed him.

"My father. My f-father never let me. . . *He made me just like him.* When mother died, *man I can't even remember her voice anymore*, he was afraid to be alone! That was it! He needed me to become this. . . *caricature* of men so I could go out in confidence and have an eight-kid-friggin'-family to make sure he always had someone. *That was so selfish!* He was so afraid I might 'turn out gay' that he named me after a *penis THREE TIMES! TELL ME THAT'S NOT COMPLETELY MESSED UP!?*" Dick was sniffling and spitting through his words, Max had never seen him like this. He must have overestimated his ability to withstand the room. *Three times though?* That didn't make sense.

"Dick, what is your full name?" Max approached the sobbing hill with an outstretched hand.

"Dickson," he inhaled, slobbering, "*Peterwilly. . .* Davison."

Max stifled a laugh that came on so suddenly it could not be stopped and he *snorted. Dickson Peterwilly Davison* returned to him a shattered look not unlike a starving boy from a charity commercial, a single tear drop taunted overwhelming sadness on the edge of a puffy eyelid.

Max Martin momentarily personified the characteristics of garbage.

It was that moment Agent Stone chose to stride up from behind them, quiet as a librarian's ghost, and *slap* Davison straight across the chin. Perhaps she chose the chin because it was an easy target, it made a heavy *THWAP* nonetheless. Dick Davison was a man in possession of the largest chin that Max had ever seen in his entire life, due to an abundance of testosterone presumably, but this thing was pushing into tumor territory. Dick snapped out of his combination of mental anguish and existential rage immediately and stood straight up like a meerkat, steadying one arm on the red fabric chair directly behind him. His eyes showed evidence of a crucial mental replay and when it was over, he looked deep into the back of Max's skull, eyes hot with murder, delivering an award-worthy pantomime depicting how a throat is slit.

And so the agents silently resumed their introspective march behind the stern blonde arbitrator that led them. When they reached the simple metal door at the end of *The Room Of Introspection*, Davison barged into the small area it preceded and headed up the spiral staircase contained within, his head down and his mind elsewhere. Before Stone could place her first foot on the wrought-iron step, though, Max tapped her shoulder and addressed her.

"Hey. He was really having a moment back there. Think you could have handled that a little more *gently?*"

"*Emotional issues.* Stop me if he breaks an arm." She brushed it off, unfazed by his appeal. Absent-mindedly she picked a purplish fibre from the waist of her long black jacket.

"*Wow.* Alright. So tell me, has there ever been a moment in the day, *any day*, that you've spent thinking about how somebody *else* feels?" Max pleaded for a reasonable response with two open hands.

"Never."

Max sighed and looked at his shoes, two of the only things in the world that, thus far, had not disappointed him. But shoes were fount of treachery, and the day would surely come.

"Perhaps that is why I'm in love with a man that hasn't reacted to my existence since learning my name." Stone spoke in a tone that was entirely unknown to him, causing Max to look back suddenly, where he caught her flinch in self-inflicted shock. She glared at him, spun, and hurried up the stair case, thin soles patting the iron stairs quickly and quietly.

Max would be glad to leave this floor. As enlightening as that experience had been, the dramatics were palpable, and he was no better at dealing with them now than he had been in high school. Looking upwards, the stairs seemed to continue for long enough to take them at least another three or four floors. That was good, but he remarked to himself how ridiculous and wasteful it all was, the construction of this building, and how the only thing needed to shut it all down was a malfunctioning elevator. Maybe it wasn't *such* a bad idea if Bilge lost his mind and sold off some assets. This building was too big and too complex for *anyone* to handle, though he sensed that this *was* not and *would* not be the only time a member of the Aversion Bureau put *that* thought together. Attempting to remember the lyrics beyond just the chorus of '*Mad World*' occupied the rest of the long climb, and the song fit the situation well. A small victory in the tiny war on boredom.

At the top of the stairs was an open door, and in the hallway beyond the door stood Agents Stone and Davison, both looking uncomfortable. "So why exactly are all the floors reached by completely different means? Has the elevator never gone out before?" Max huffed from his climb and attempted to change the subject in the back of everyone's minds.

"The empty building was built first, all of the rooms and floors piece by piece as they were dreamt up. The Bureau has been a work in progress for as long as it has been. You'll need to remember that when Director Bilge built this place, he was still obscenely rich," Explained Agent Stone coolly. She did not look at him but addressed the hallway, trying to remember it.

"Yeah, alright, but a ladder and then a staircase just seem a little boring is all," said Max, imagining the superior number of Jacuzzis and chocolate statues of nude women he would have installed given similar circumstances; perhaps another elevator also.

"Don't worry bro, next one will be better." Dick managed a half-smile, then returned to his thoughts. Stone set off to the right and down the hall, blue and white tile, pale walls and a generally higher level of upkeep than the previous floors defined the scene.

"Floor thirty-one. One of the research floors. Labs and scientists, not much else. I know the way, we'll find Agent Andersen's lab here. Fix the elevator. *Go home.* We follow the hall until it ends." She instructed commandingly while the men followed behind her. There were closed doors with frosted windows spaced equally along the walls, labeled with the names of various important people with doctorates and degrees in this and that. Most all of them bore bold black signs that read *SOLD* and *FOR SALE* in obnoxious neon letters, this floor seemed hard-hit by Director Bilge's classified ad from earlier. They approached a left-hand bend in the path with yet another closed wooden door situated before the junction. This door, however, flew open when they approached it. A dark skinned man in a well-worn lab coat emerged from it, his wiry beard was shocked with white and speckled with vomit. He looked back and spat at the door's sign which now swung free from one of its scotch-tape hinges. His blood-shot eyes moved more slowly than did his head, and he inspected the agents sluggishly.

"Ahm lookin' fer *Shally*."

"*Sally*." Agent Stone re-pronounced the name. The piss-faced scientist grunted angrily and pointed with a nearly-empty bottle of rum, which previously had appeared to be a normal part of his arm, towards the sign dangling from the door. He thrusted with his bottle for inflection.

"F-O-R-SAL-E." His first attempt met with zero recognition from the sober people.

"*FOR. SALLY.*" He threw his arms up in the air as if to pull conclusions out of God's own ass.

"*Whosh Sally!?*" His weathered hands now mimicked typing. "I gots a mail on the computer this mornin'. *Six years* of work out the poop tube, cuz some broad *Sally's* gettin' every *science box* and research *projikt* in THAT ROOM. So I asks ya, *whoose Sally?*" Red rage and liquor madness pulsed below the skin of his face.

Agent Stone hesitated, unsure of how to proceed. Davison didn't hardly seem to acknowledge what was going on, he just stood, looking sad. Seeing this, Max took the initiative.

"What the hell," he stepped forward and said with a shrug, "*I'm Sally.*"

Doctor rum-bottle dropped his namesake and dove towards him, grabbing a fistful of red tie with one hand and digging into his coat pocket with the other. Max tried to dodge but tripped up on a loose shoe-lace. *Et tu, shoe*? The drunken scientist produced a large remote with a comically over-sized red button in the center and held it above their heads, menacing with it.

"YOU *BISCH! Do you even Science?! Why don't I just press this huge button and kills us all?*" The Scientist drew Max to ninety-percent of kissing distance. The arm of his lab coat was covered in animal hair. His breath was poison. "*If I presh this button, we're all as good as dead! That is why it is large and red, to make the proshpect of pressing it seem heavy. . . with conshequensh.*"

"A-actually has kind of the opposite effect," he gagged on his attacker's putrid liquor exhalings.

"*I could do it, Sally. I could do it and even your famoush beauty couldn't stop me. . .*"

Agent Max Martin put his heel into the increasingly unlikeable man's shin and dropped to the floor, breaking his grasp. As he knew she would, Agent Stone stepped up and brought her fist through the fool's jaw, putting him down in a single blow. He collapsed weightily and the remote he was holding launched theatrically in a grand arc towards the ceiling, rotating rapidly and falling back down again to land directly on the infamous red button, which *clicked* audibly as it depressed.

"What do you know," said Sally bitterly. "Buttered-side down."

The sound of a very large shutter drawing up and opening rumbled from the doorway in front of them, too dark and far inside to see. Stone spoke as she helped Max to his feet. "I believe this was a situation pre-arranged to result in our failure."

"A trap?" he offered.

"Sure."

Heavy footsteps infused with the clacking of nails were the only sounds now, a hulking shape came towards the door from inside the room and rattled the walls with each step. Stone readied herself for combat and Max looked over at her, attempting to mimic her position in hopes that it would help him too. First came a great hooked beak, ducking low to fit under the door, followed by five feet of thickly feathered neck and the stout body of a steroid-abusing professional ostrich. The beast struggled to stand at its full height in the hallway, so it crouched, the massive bird's head tilted to provide vision to black eyes set on either side of its head. It soon noticed the liquor-soaked scientist sprawled on the floor and grabbed him in its beak, choking the body down like an owl devouring a mouse. . . only this was not an owl, but instead an eight-foot tall blue-feathered monster wholly devouring a fully-grown, mentally unwell human male. Max gulped hard, to get his testicles to drop back down to their usual space.

"*Tesla raptors.* Thought we had the last ones euthanized.," said Agent Stone, visibly tense.

The feathered horror finished its meal and turned opal eyes to the agents, opening its jagged beak in a flash and producing a tremendous violet light from within. A beam of sparking, electric death blasted from the raptor's gullet, narrowly avoiding the nearly catatonic Dick Davison leaning against a wall, whilst the other two agents leapt to either side. The violet lightning erupted down the hall, scorching the floor. Agent Stone directed the beasts' attention with a sharp clap and Agent Martin yelped something about not having guns in a voice that cracked with fear. The raptor clacked its beak at the tiny morsel, testing its reach. Stone spun a kick that struck it on the jaw sending its head *smacking* into the wall of hallway. The hallway's lack of room to maneuver would be an advantage for the physically inferior humans. A thick wet tongue lolled from the side of the bird's open beak. Stone took a step towards it and struck for its eye with a closed fist, the tree-trunk neck snaked away and came back in a savage whip, but the agent rolled underneath. Meanwhile, Max Martin found his courage and picked the empty rum bottle from the floor. He came on, bringing it up to the creature's chin, smashing the glass and producing the first droplets of blood. A squawk of dismay bled out and it shifted in a few short steps to bring feathery fury down on the miniscule man with the massive hair. But this was a feint, and not by the soft little combatants. Stone was using the distraction to step into striking range of this creature's notoriously fragile collarbone when it broke away from Max and struck back towards her, unexpectedly hammering Stone with a closed beak as large as her torso. She flew backwards and hit the wall hard.

Max looked on in horror, then noticed his friend and colleague Dick Davison, the only man capable of physically matching this beast, looking onto the carnage so lost in his own worries that he did not react to his partner's cry of pain as she collapsed to the floor.

"Dickson *Peterwilly* Davison!" Max bellowed at

the top of his unremarkable lung capacity. Davison met his eyes but otherwise remained unchanged.

"*You are no bro of mine,*" he hissed.

Max whistled, poorly, and the tesla raptor reeled on him, still salivating at the meal he almost made of Agent Stone. It tilted its head curiously at his un-concerning threat. Max struck high with a strong punch and impressively managed to bruise his hand *and* wrist simultaneously on the bird's concrete beak. It coiled backwards and struck out, snake-like, with open jaws. Max brought up his left arm to protect himself and so was it caught in the bite. He shouted as the gargantuan jaws put pressure on his arm and pulled back. He felt his shoulder lose grip of the socket and a blinding flash of pain followed a heavy snap in his forearm. Max closed his eyes and clenched his teeth. *Die a hero, and it will all be worth it.* This was his last thought.

Or it would have been, but suddenly, the pressure released. Agent Martin opened his eyes and saw his friend and saviour drawing the demon beak apart with bare hands and ridiculous bronze biceps. Max pulled away from the mouth and his wet-sleeved arm flopped to his side, the pain currently muted by adrenaline. Dick Davison grunted and *threw* the bird's head into the floor where the two halves of beak CLACKED as they bounced off of the tile. Max jogged to his beaten partner and pulled her to her feet with his good hand. She regarded Davison with a solemn nod and he reciprocated. As the raptor dizzily attempted to raise its head, Dick slammed it back to the ground with an over-head axe handle of inhuman force.

"I'll hold it off. You guys go," he panted.

"*NEVER!*" barked Max, "*that's too cliché!*"

Just then Dick was smacked into by a head butt from the desperate animal. He absorbed it and grasped the creature's beak, holding it back against the ground with concentrated effort.

"What's wrong with clichés, bro? Is *HEROISM* cliché? A cliché becomes what it is because people like to see that kind of thing!" There was nothing but seriousness in his tone. The two beasts struggled against each other's might.

"Besides, familiarity is comforting!" Davison released his grip temporarily, to deliver a devastating left hook that sent the Tesla Raptor toppling over. Sabre-like claws skittered on the floor and it squawked noisily in defiance.

"If you insist!" Max said. He supported Stone on his right arm as they made off to continue down the hall and past the madness. From behind them, the beast loudly succumbed to animalist rage and plowed into Davison full force, the two of them disappeared down the bend of hallway the group had originally come from.

"*I do!*" Davison shouted to him, optimism in his voice. Strain in his breathing.

Max shook the doubt from his mind and let Agent Stone lead him to their goal. They reached another bend of the hallway and took it until there was nowhere else to go. A supply closet of incredibly familiar design sat in the wall at the end. They stopped in front of it, Max with his back to the door. His partner looked as though she had just come from a vigorous boxing match, and not a near-deadly brush with a monstrous lab animal. She was bruised and ragged, but otherwise completely composed.

"Agent Davison was right, you know. If you ever want to become a great agent of the Aversion Bureau, you're going to have begin embracing clichés," she told him.

Max looked down at his limp left arm, the one he nearly lost moments ago. As he began to focus on it again, it began to hurt. With great pain and struggle he formed that hand into a fist. . .

"*I will avenge him.*"

"See, there you go."

Stone looked over his shoulder, clearly recognizing this particular janitor's roost. "Is your arm broken?" she asked him, looking only past him.

"Shit. I think so." Max winced at it.

"*Then hold very still. . .*"

She shoved him by the chest, backwards through the door as it swung open to let him through. Suddenly Max was falling, gliding on his back like a greasy prostitute during a special house call. Was this a *slide,* he wondered, as long black hair whipped over his face. *They weren't kidding, this IS more fun than a staircase.* Max spun around to his belly, holding his now-vestigial seeming arm carefully in place. Ignoring the growing ache, he managed a chuckle of fun; what stretched before him was a rapidly approaching spot of light marking the end of the dark slide. It was on him as soon as he had seen it and Max reacted without thinking, bracing the sudden impact with *both* hands, his vision flashed colourless and he *heaved* the contents of his stomach onto the concrete floor. Nothing came up though, the events of the day hadn't even allowed for a visit to the vending machine - let alone breakfast. Max rose slowly to his feet feeling sick, dizzy and delirious from pain. He had absolutely no idea where the ride had taken him, and he didn't care. A drifting painless death surrounded by loved ones would be fantastic right about now, he figured. It always looked good in the movies.

It was then that Agent Stone whooshed in from the slide and deftly avoided him in a spectacular landing well deserving of playground adulation. She bent down, tore a long strip of fabric from her white pant leg and fashioned Max a makeshift sling, which she then tied for him. A nice match for the bandage on his forehead. While she set his broken arm he tried to vomit on her in self-defense, until he realized what she was doing. Her pants looked ridiculous now, why did she do that?

"There," she said, "try not to throw any more punches. *Maybe forever.*"

". . . and also, good work up there," Stone added. She seemed to be in a good mood. This was somehow the *strangest* thing he'd seen all day. *Why would she be in a good mood?* Max stopped caring about this particular mystery though, as soon as he felt a fresh spike of pain from his shoulder. Dislocated AND broken. This is what happens when you keep a *three-leaf* clover in your wallet out of laziness.

"Where are we?" He blinked at his surroundings. So many sources of light, maybe he was finally *backstage.*

"Agent Andersen's lab. He's behind us right now at his desk, follow me." She pulled him along by the good hand. Indeed there were many sources of light, though few were bright enough to make his surroundings anything better than dim. They showed, though, that this was a smaller room than most; the room was shaped like a large letter 'T'. Max saw dozens upon dozens of monitors and strips of blinking lights decorating plain concrete walls, along with densely loaded tables and shelves all storing fragments of technology. It was cluttered, but not messy. Colour of any kind was sparse here, only blue light and grey plastics. The pair stopped in the center of the room, in front of an expansive multi-branching desk with a very

41

large, very round man sitting in the center, typing away at his keyboard and giving not a moment of recognition to either of them. Stone was strangely quiet, so Max spoke first.

"*Hey Wade.*"

Agent Wade Andersen nodded, his eyes never leaving his screen.

"Agent Andersen," she finally said to him, her voice uneven. He stopped typing, turned his round pale face and made eye contact with her, his expression remained blank. His expression was *always* blank. Agent Andersen was of the most impossibly *neutral* demeanor every single moment that Max had ever seen him. Where some men were men of few words, Wade Andersen was primarily a man of *zero and or one* words.

"W-we, we've come about the. . . *the thing*. The s-small moving room." Agent Stone stumbled through a mouthy obstacle course where a single word would have sufficed. Max watched her fail, and watched her eyes. They couldn't meet Wade's, not for more than a second before darting away. She was sweating and he noticed.

"Elevator," Andersen offered, still as stone.

"Yeah Wade, the elevator, obviously, she's out of words I guess." Max stepped in to the conversation, exasperated with his colleague.

"Used them all last night," said Wade. Max

adopted a scandalized expression and leaned in to look closer at Agent Stone, she noticed the look he was giving her and turned her head down. She was *blushing*. Today was full of surprises indeed.

"Heavily intoxicated then. Extremely distracting."

Agent Stone released air from her lungs, none of this air reminded anyone of words.

Max Martin sighed loudly and rubbed the bridge of his nose. "*Nobody has time for this.* Wade, can you fix the stupid elevator so we can get up to the stupid fifty-first-stupid-God-damn floor and *end this?*"

"Of course."

"*Will you?*"

"No."

Max wasn't sure what to say, but his partner found her tongue.

"Agent Andersen you *must* help us stop Bilge's madness. The Bureau cannot survive a further moment of his *insanity* and you know that." Max nodded along with her words. Wade listened to her, then turned to his computer, and clicked the mouse twice.

"Behold insanity." Wade spoke, pushing away from this desk on a rolling chair, turning ninety degrees to offer them a look at his rather large computer screen.

They walked around the table and stood next to him to see. Wade Andersen kept an immaculate workspace, there were two of every doodad and three of every gizmo. Every piece was in perfect order except for in the far corner of the desk where there was a nest of discarded papers below a dangling, frayed Ethernet cable for some reason. Agent Andersen's long sleeved grey-green shirt and black vest were bathed blue in the light of the monitor as he looked at them, awaiting their reaction to what the computer presented. A file was open on the screen, the receipt for a charitable donation. This morning, roughly an hour before the epic quest to stop him had begun, Director Bilge had apparently donated *ten-thousand dollars* to a United Kingdom-based charity for "*The Betterment of Children with Bloody Awful Luck.*" Max was pleasantly surprised. If this is what Bilge had been doing all day, he thought, it was actually pretty cool.

"Wildly irresponsible expenditures!" Stone protested. "Did you know that he's also been auctioning off important lab and research equipment on the *internet!?*"

Wade gave *his* lab a cursory inspection, from door, to ridiculous slide-entrance, to elevator.

"Not mine," he said.

Agent Stone was growing agitated by his reluctance to concede. "Max got his arm broken just now! Because a degenerate, insane scientist unleashed his monstrous *pet* on us!" She stabbed the air around Max's sling with an angry finger. One so often forgets the location of arms simply described.

"Non-fatal," Wade diagnosed, looking at Max. He waved his chubby hand under a spout-bearing dispenser sitting on his desk. Two white pills popped out with a whirring noise, he offered them to Max. Who happily swallowed them dry before asking what they were. "What are these?" He asked.

"Pills," Wade returned.

Max raised an eyebrow and opened his mouth to try again.

"*Arm pills.*" Stone brushed him off and readied another argument. "Why aren't you working with me? Why won't you help us?"

"Because," Wade Andersen began. A strand of platinum blonde hair came loose from one of the curls clustering his head and landed right in front of his cold blue eyes. It caused no reaction. "My bread knows the origins of its butter."

Then the computer behind them dinged. A *happy* ding, the ding of fresh mail. Wade spun back to it and read the message. Unsurprisingly, he did this in his head, so Max and his partner peeked over Wade's huge shoulders to see for themselves. Agent Stone leaned closer in than did Max and Wade shifted away to compensate. She read aloud:

"*Attention staff of the Aversion Bureau. Chaps, blokes and mates of the Bureau included also. A lucrative deal with an international book publisher has been reached today and I will be requiring henceforth that each and every one of you surrender any and all personal writings, journals and or diaries to me at once. On penalty of discharge. Have a smashing afternoon!*

-Sincerely, Director Thomas Bilge."

"Oh, look at that. Insanity is suddenly relative, it seems." Agent Stone spoke directly into Andersen's expressionless face. "I know about your diaries Wade, and so I wonder what you say to our pleas now?"

"Regicide," said Wade. He opened a desk drawer and produced a large antennae bearing knife-switch labeled *ELEVATOR SYSTEM*, It was currently set to *OFF*. He grabbed her hand and placed it on the handle of the switch. Stone lost all composure at the touch but coughed it away and slammed the switch to the coveted position of *NOT OFF*.

"I say regicide."

Agent Stone walked away from the table satisfied, perhaps *too* satisfied. Agent Martin tasted bile in his mouth, whether it was from her behaviour or his gradually swelling appendage in the sling he honestly didn't know. She patted the good half of his back.

"We're back on schedule Agent. Go to the big closet and pick yourself out something nice. My treat."

Max looked around and found the big closet almost immediately, next to the elevator at the far end of the lab. Grey, metal and as promised, *big*.

"Andersen is your coffee machine working?" Stone walked to a table in the back of the room.

"Affirmative."

Max was halfway finished waddling sorely to the closet when he heard that.

"My God, *PLEASE* bring me a cup. These *arm pills* are tearing up my stomach." And they were. Max reached the large closet and flung it open to a wonderful sight. *Guns*. Guns and a small selection of knives, though according to the warning labels they carried, *never* to be brought against each other in a fight. Agent Martin had received training with almost all of the weapons before him. Though he was complete crap with everything except a basic pistol, nothing erased the constant fear of letting women down sexually than waving a huge friggin' shotgun around. As he window-shopped though, he remembered why he needed a gun at all. Or rather, why he *didn't*. They were heading upstairs to potentially *fight* Director Bilge, who was by all *sober* accounts a kindly and generous old man and a pretty good boss. The same old man, in fact, who just this morning had clearly donated thousands of dollars to unlucky British kids. Drunken, tyrannical stupor or no, that didn't seem like a man you pointed a gun at. He chose nothing.

Agent Stone appeared behind him and reached over his shoulder to remove a long katana from the case, something he hadn't noticed there beforehand. It was all black and unadorned, save for a silver 'S' on the hilt. *For 'sword', h*e pieced together. He knew Agent Stone to be a master sword fighter, and felt safer seeing her with one again. Ideally, she could just disarm Bilge in the coming battle instead of slicing him in half. But he wouldn't get his hopes up. She reached in once more and removed a decidedly more ornate weapon, a silver breech-loaded shotgun with enameled roses and a worn wooden stock. She caught Max looking at it and answered his mute question. "For Davison."

"*If he. . .*"

"Yeah."

The two of them walked over to the now-working elevator door. From this view of the room, Max could see the half-empty, still brewing coffee pot at the other end. His stomach grumbled and he suddenly realized that Stone had never brought him that cup of coffee he asked for. Max was about to inquire after it but was interrupted by a last minute appeal from their fellow agent at the desk.

"Agents." He did not raise his voice. "Advice."

Stone called the elevator and they turned to hear him.

"You rush headlong to audience with a mad king."

"We do," she answered him.

He paused for effect.

"Expect madness."

Stone and Martin nodded in acknowledgement. The elevator had arrived, so they walked inside and turned to face Agent Wade Andersen. Even to the closing of the door he watched them, silently.

"Sweet holy *Hell,* Wade is a weird guy." Max let out in a quick breath, imagining himself out of earshot. Agent Stone elbowed him lightly in his broken arm and for the third time today he fruitlessly heaved in pain. Max slumped to the floor of the elevator to get away from her and tried to change the subject as the small, moving room stuttered into upwards motion. He looked at the shotgun she was holding and felt worry tying a fresh knot in his stomach.

"You really think he's going to make it?" Max asked.

Agent Stone just stared down at him, delivering her classic look of condescension. As though planned, their ride unexpectedly stopped there. Only one floor up from Wade's lab where they left mere sentences ago. The door opened and a man stepped in: a giant of a man, burned, bloodied, and bruised. But smiling. Strangely enough, he was already holding a shotgun of his own.

"Had to remember where I hid this one to deal with that big-ass chicken." He kissed it loudly. "I love you, boom-stick."

Max would have jumped to greet his friend but had no energy left for it, so he simply allowed himself to relax. "Hey little bro!" Davison beamed artificially whitened teeth down at him and messed up his black, all-consuming hair. "Miss me?"

"More than you'd be comfortable with," said Max. Dick didn't know how to process that, so he turned to the other agent.

"I brought you this," she said, offering him the fancier shotgun. Dick whistled and tossed his beloved 'boom-stick' between the closing elevator doors. It clattered loudly away. Max was flabbergasted and gestured accordingly.

"A man who has loved but once, has never truly loved," explained Agent Davison, cocking his new gun-wife repeatedly just to hear the sound she made. "You'll learn that when you're older." A shotgun shell clinked onto the floor, and the ride continued in silence for a while until Dick noticed Agent Stone adjusting the shoulder-strap of her sheathed sword.

"*Oooh* you grabbed the Katana. Classic," he said.

"Any other day a mere *Katana*." She unsheathed the blade, allowing it to ring.

"Tonight, the sword of Damocles. . ."

Davison regarded her with a punch on the arm.

"*Sick reference bro.*"

PHASE THREE

The elevator carried the agents gradually upwards, a peristaltic climb through the esophagus of a great concrete bird regurgitating justice into the gaping mouths of waiting sinners.

Riding to the fifty-first floor took a long time.

The Agents Stone and Davison stood with their weapons at the ready, while Max sat on the floor cradling his swollen, broken arm. It was aching, but getting better already thanks to the pills that Wade had given him, whatever they were. Max pulled his surprisingly undamaged phone from his pocket and checked the time, pleased to find that the entirety of this adventure had so far only cost them two hours of the day. He was happy about that, it was good to know that when all of this was over, there would still be enough time to go home and sit on the internet for six hours. He realized something else as well, looking at a recent missed call notification belonging to his roommate. This internet-capable texting device in his hand had the miraculous capability to send and receive recordings of the human voice. The realization hit him like a Frisbee with the sun behind it.

"Why didn't we call him?" Max sat straight up and spoke to Agent Stone specifically. "Why the hell didn't we just *call* Wade and try to convince him to restart the elevator over the phone?!"

She looked at him, then away from him, frowning. "Agent Andersen *has* my phone number. . . on a *list* of numbers. . . that are *blocked*." It came forth with difficulty.

Max was undeterred. "No! With MY phone! It's still got a charge, see?" He held it up and wiggled it, to prove that it had electricity inside. "We could have avoided the part of the day where I almost got my arm eaten." His tone was not friendly.

Agent Stone still looked straight ahead and would not react to him, instead she cleared her throat and fussed with her sleeves. "I may *also* have figured out how to call him from *your* phone number. . . *and* Agent Davison's. . . and the director's." Dick laughed at her but Max sunk back slowly, just imagining his colleague in the jaws of a massive demon-bird, with no last minute rescue at hand, *dying apologetically.*

"Also a number I found on a bathroom stall once. He didn't see that one coming," Stone added.

BING!

The elevator had been practicing its one line at the turn of every floor with a small *boop,* preparing for this moment, and now they were there. The fifty-first floor. The elevator door here opened directly into Director Bilge's office. Max had seen this office several dozen times in two years, and when he turned his head to have a look, somewhat anticlimactically, it was exactly the same and as orderly as always. It had been cleaned since last the party last night. Agents Stone and Davison took a step in unison into the large square office, Dick holding his classy shotgun high and Stone cracking her knuckles. The walls were painted off-white and dark-varnished wood made up the cabinet and chairs inside. A blue strip of carpet lead them like a runway from the elevator to the two chairs that sat in front of the director's wide, plain desk. There were a handful of potted plants inside the room and to their right, humongous window-walls illuminated everything with noonday sun. The windows showed just how high they were at the top of this building. Pine forest stretched as far as the eye could see and grey mountains backed them at the edge of sight. A view for a king.

Bilge was at his desk, Max saw, looking through tiny half-moon reading glasses at his laptop and absently fingering the handle of a tremendous ceramic jug. A name plate and lone stuffed animal sat on the desk next to him, a little goat-bear. Behind him, a massive plaque of the symbol of the Aversion Bureau was mounted. From here, Max thought, it looked more like a seventy-one.

"Waiting for us?" Stone asked him, from across the room.

Director Thomas Bilge put a hand on his laptop and closed it, looked towards his agents.

"I watch everything my dear, but I wait for nothing."

He spoke with a thick British accent, Max didn't know where he was from specifically, and wherever it was wasn't spelled the same way it was pronounced anyway.

The elevator door was about to close, Max realized. He shot up to his feet and stepped out into the room, immediately feeling the effect of the pills in a new way. His legs were meat-flavoured gelatin and his head felt like it was half-way filled with wet plaster. He careened towards the back of agent Davison's massive body, but sidestepped him and stumbled immediately back down to the floor, inside the room, planting his ass against the wall right next to the elevator door. There he resigned to make this friendly plant pot beside him into a companion, as well as an arm rest. He thanked it for being there.

"*Maxwell*, boy, are you on *the drugs?*" Max

heard legitimate concern in his boss's voice. As if he wasn't perfectly aware of what they had run into downstairs.

Pfffffft.

Max momentarily amused himself with the noises his mouth could make. "*Apparently!* I broke my arm dodging all the wacky *bullshit* you set up to stop us from getting here!"

Bilge frowned at the accusation, about to speak. But instead Dick Davison spoke, striding confidently and slowly across the room to Bilge's desk, tapping the long silver shotgun methodically against his shoulder. Bilge pushed back from his chair and rose to make eye contact. They were almost of a height; Thomas Bilge had always also been a very large man, though a swollen belly and comfortable sweater now belied the director's lifetime spent in Britain's Special Air Service. Max looked from one to the other, both men had tremendous, strong *chins*. Dick's was boxy, Bilge's was clean shaven and nigh-polygonal. Max felt very *jaw conscious* as he rubbed the rounded contours of his own.

"Now, we've done this dance before, *bossbro*, you get blasted and hole up in your office. You make wild purchases with our pensions and salaries, nearly destroy the company, and we head up here to stop you." Dick raised the shotgun and gestured with the barrel, all towards Bilge. "The only difference, is that *this* time. . . the three of us almost *died*." Dick was letting his anger show, his easy smile was fire.

"That is far from the only difference." Thomas Bilge was unflinching in the face of this threat, his extreme, bushy, pure-white mustache and shaved head made him look a funny combination of bar-room brawler and Santa Claus. His eyes were ice.

"*Stop this* – " Dick started but Bilge spoke commandingly over him. "Stop *what?* Dearest Davison, never point your weapon towards any animal *NOR* man unless you truly believe you will be able kill it." Dick shrunk, the smallest amount, and lowered his shotgun arm. "Now are you really upset with me or are you very much acting out of disappointment. I saw you on the cameras, last night, with all of those women on the twentieth floor. *Sales*, lad, I saw what happened in *sales*. Nine drunken women threw themselves at you that night, and you touched. . . not a *single* one. . . so went the '*Sex Orchestra*'." Bilge snorted, but it was the only hint of mocking he allowed. "Why do you feel the need to lie to yourself?"

"I. . . needed someone to talk to." Dick softened, his fierceness momentarily extinguished. But then he caught himself. "*STOP IT. Don't change the subject! You know why we came here bro!!*" Davison whipped his gun up to point it at the old man again.

"I do." Thomas Bilge sighed.

BANG

Bilge *booted*, with one slippered foot, his entire mahogany desk a foot and a half across the carpeted floor and sent it crashing into his employee's unsuspecting pelvis. Dick Davison was knocked clear off his feet, crushed a wooden chair with the back of his head upon landing, and went to sleep for the rest of the day.

"That poor boy has some issues to work out." Bilge dusted himself off. He wore beige shorts and a woolen sweater with a design knit from many shades of blue, a small kitten, asleep under a tree. Director Bilge was famous for his sweaters, he wore a different one every single day of his life, every one of them was colourful and every one of them looked damn comfortable. Max was shocked by his cold efficiency, but completely enthralled, and the texture of the carpeting in this room was *utterly fantastic* as well.

"Now, *Natalie,* my dear, will *you* listen to me?" She flinched at the address. Bilge bent down to retrieve that massive ceramic jug he had just sent toppling off his desk and lifted it with one hand. It must have been almost empty to not spill in the carnage, but whatever was left didn't last long. Bilge wiped his mouth and tossed it aside. Agent Stone stepped slowly to meet him in the centre of the room, keeping a good six feet of wary distance. Max had never heard her first name used before, she would never allow herself to be called by it. But now he knew what it was, and couldn't resist. Max giggled the giggle of a man discovering bad words in good places.

". . . *Natalie?* That's *pretty.*" She shot him a look more fierce than any he had ever received from her. Honestly the mean looks were getting a bit old, but he knew the drill. Max punched himself in the swollen arm and sat silently again. Twiddling his left thumb manually.

"I don't know what happened to you down there, or *why*, but I have been *immensely* busy since last night." Thomas Bilge began explaining to her, with pleading eyes, "I am very drunk, perhaps more drunk than I've ever been, and only *now* am I truly sober. Any dreams can become reality, they teach us, but they must be dreamt in the sleep of day, and acted on, in *inebriation.* Now I have woken! The sobriety I speak of, *man's true state of mind*, actually requires an astonishing amount of booze. . ."

"The words of a drunk." Agent Stone dismissed him, and slowly drew the katana from her shoulder sheathe. She brandished her blade in the sun and *smiled*, for the first time all day. Max sat there, head spinning, still completely lost in the meta.

"Last night I went *beyond* the mortal drunken madness we all know and love. I reached another *state of being* and since then I have come to realize *so much.* This morning alone I have donated thirty-thousand dollars of my personal estate to a string of charities that I know to be truly deserving. That has been more fulfilling than any work I've done in the decade we've spent working in this organization."

Agent Stone polished the sword with her long black coat.

"How have we never seen it before? *The whole bloody thing is a joke!* The chocolate factory is made of gold and all it produces pales! Surely, we *do* help people when I send you agents on your missions. The backwoods nursery attacked by mountain giants? *Davison was needed.* The oil patch workers nearly eaten by mole people? *Your skills were required.* The self-made cyborg hacker who shut down his small town's electrical grid? *Agent Martin shot that man.*

These situations are few and far between, and there are older organizations better suited to these tasks. That is why the layman doesn't even know that monsters *do* exist. *Who are we then?* We have saved many lives, and even undeniably bettered our small area of the world with our efforts. But the cost of running this organization balanced against the good we're truly capable of is the difference between the elephant and the mouse. I am frightened of the truth. The truth that we may be playing a game of heroes where no maidens exist." Bilge was emotional, he had the look of a guilty man as he spoke.

Agent Stone did not react. She twirled her blade, and lowered it towards him, balancing on the foot with the ripped white pant leg, preparing to fight. Max couldn't believe what he was seeing, even now, during the pill's down time. The arm pills were affecting him in waves. . . and it was *marvelous*.

"I have spent the day selling our extraneous equipment, firing our unneeded staff and turning a profit from the pure *bollocks* I have littered our halls with. I have taken this money and moved it into organizations and charities that can make more change in the world than we could ever dream of. *Because it is right!*" Bilge yelled his crimes passionately, and Max was completely taken along with him.

Max threw his good hand into the air at Agent Stone. "*Are you even listening to him?! Is this what we've been trying to STOP all day? He's making perfect damn sense! It's a money pit!*" He sat up and protested at her, gesturing wildly, but the motion made him feel dizzy so he slouched back against the wall.

Natalie Stone shook her head and again, smiled. "I dared to believe in the Bureau."

Bilge tensed and his eyes narrowed. He reached a hand slowly down to his flipped desk.

"Who dares wins. Come then, my girl."

She rushed at him and swung down hard. From the underside of his desk, Bilge produced a magnificent steel sabre and brought it up just in time to catch her blade. The swords banged together, and he turned hers away. Stone jumped back to dodge his return fire. Max was witnessing Agent Stone, whom he now believed to be *truly insane*, sword-fight a man who perhaps was the most sane individual in the building at this time. Max drank shame and fear together in an emotion cocktail, now amplified by the return of the arm pills. She couldn't dare hurt him, not after everything he'd said. Bilge was the only one thinking clearly this whole time, It had turned out. Then Bilge opened his mouth and bellowed a chilling war-scream before advancing again on his employee, swinging and slashing with his metal arm. At that, Max realized that these two were equally insane, and perhaps perfectly suited for each other. He gave up on having opinions and allowed the situation to unfold.

Bilge checked her blows with his massive sabre, but Stone delivered them more quickly and took a narrow strip of fabric from his pant leg. They looked as though they might honestly kill each other. Natalie slashed high and Bilge ducked, he spun and brought his blade in a massive sweeping cut to her legs. She jumped over it. After returning two flashing cuts to his sides, Stone stepped back once more. They were standing right in front of Max now. The arm pills allowed very little extra energy for fearing death, so he watched them, glassy-eyed and amused. Both fighters were clearly beginning to tire. Fat beads of sweat poured from Bilge's brow, he was impossibly swift for his size, but was still an old man. Bilge stumbled on his next attack, rushing forward with a weighty over handed swing. Agent Stone was ready, she moved in from below and caught his sword with her own, holding it horizontally above her head, she stepped close, sweeping both blades out and away. She dropped her sword, and in one fluid motion pulled *something* from her jacket pocket and *stabbed* Thomas Bilge directly in the fat of his sweater shielded stomach. Not with a blade though, Max saw that what she used was instead a syringe. A syringe of rapidly disappearing *black* liquid.

Coffee.

The adrenaline of witnessing an almost-murder brought Max back into it. "*Is that SAFE?!*"

Natalie smiled one final time, right at him. "Safer than a sword fight."

And for perhaps the first time in his life, Max Martin was silent. Director Thomas Bilge dropped his chinked sabre and slumped. Stone caught his weight and moved his arm over her shoulder. There were a few long moments before Bilge came back to them, then he perked up and looked around scared, like a man waking up in a hospital bed. She wiped a crown of sweat from his brow.

"Natalie girl. . . am I?"

"Sober. Let's get you home, we'll clean all of this up in the morning." She spoke so softly, Max could forget that they had almost killed each other in front of him just minutes ago. Agent Stone limped to the door with a walrus on her arm. When he realized that they were literally just going to *leave* after all of this, he couldn't pick a single question from all the ones that bashed around in his mouth. Max realized that it didn't matter what he understood in the end, because at least in this circumstance, he still had his job. So he just raised his good hand in the air. Stone noticed, and turned.

"Yes Agent. Any questions?"

"Just one." He turned the hand into a finger and pointed at his bandaged forehead, never leaving her eyes. "I wanna know how I got this scar. From last night? Tell me it was heroic."

"Oh yes, that. You tripped in the parking lot last night, following me out. I found you still sleeping there when I returned to the Bureau in the morning. That's all," she informed him matter-of-factly. *At least she didn't laugh.*

Max turned his pointing hand into a little bird and showed it to her, she nodded in acceptance and turned to leave.

"Good-day Max! I'll see you bright and early in a few days. Have a lovely weekend!" Bilge waved back to him and beamed as they reached the elevator. He really was a kind man and an excellent boss. Perhaps a little later, he would remember his liquored-up revelation and finish what he started. Max almost wished for that, but wouldn't bet a dime on it. Even so, the rest of this just didn't make a lot of sense. Director Thomas Bilge, he could believe, would drink himself silly and do something weird, but never would he actively set out to hurt any of them. No matter how enthralled he had become with his new purpose, it just didn't *sound* like him. The broken elevator, the nipple-zapping robots, *the room of rampant emotional issues. . .* and that mad scientist with his bird *especially* couldn't have been Bilge's fault. That guy had something else entirely going on.

Max sat there slumped against the wall, leaning his arm against his friend, the large potted plant. He found peace in the quiet office. Even if it looked an awful lot like a warzone, the carnage of battle hadn't done much to detract from the room. It really *was* tastefully done. He looked over to his other friend, *Dickson Peterwilly Davison*, passed out underneath Bilge's heavy upturned desk and snoring peacefully. Max felt the warmth of the sun on his face, and closed his eyes.

"Don't bother waking up buddy. There's nothing to see."

PHASE THREE-POINT-FIVE

A furry shape rustled in the plant-pot to the right of Max, disturbing his brief and well-earned nap time.

"Wow, I really thought we were done here," Max grumbled, reluctantly opening his eyes.

Standing now, arching its back on four skinny legs was an orange, stripy cat. He look over and let out a massive yawn which hit Max in the face with the pungent odour of bourbon and freshly-licked ass. The stretching beast hopped down silently from the big clay pot and stood to the side of Max's legs. This was Agent Whiskers, and Max was too exhausted to be surprised.

Agent Whiskers was no pet, but rather a fully-fledged and weathered agent of the Aversion Bureau, a long-con undercover agent, reconnaissance man, and kind of a jerk. Often away from the Bureau for work, Whiskers never announced his return, he would always just kind of *show up*. He wore a stylish red collar, it had a metal ring, but nothing hung there.

"What's up, kid?" Agent whiskers spoke to him, possessing the capacity for speech.

"Trying to sleep. Nearly died today. Bilge went nuts again, got drunk and raised money for charity. Set a bunch of traps so we wouldn't stop him, but we did," Max recited.

"Did he now? Last bit doesn't *sound* like him." Whiskers climbed into Agent Martin's lap, leaving hair on his black pants. Max gave him a sideways look for his odd choice of words. Agent Whiskers smiled up at him, the wicked smile of a sinister animal. This little bastard had been in Bilge's office all night, Max could only assume. *What did that mean?* And then it hit him, like a second Frisbee thrown shortly after recovering from the first.

". . .*You* got him that drunk," Max gasped, "But *why* did *you* convince him to donate all his money?" Whiskers gave him a confused look and laughed a dry laugh. It could have been a hairball.

"A man need not be generous himself to benefit

from generosity. A whisper in the ear won't change a man's nature, I merely *dangled my string*. He did what *he* wanted, *and* what I wanted. Then I just needed to make sure it didn't end too soon." The cat looked at Max's sling. "Sorry 'bout that."

Max shuddered. The little agent in his lap smiled again and rolled over to receive a scratching. Agent Martin leaned back against the wall, got comfortable and began to pet his colleague. The devil was real, and his tummy was very soft indeed.

"*This is fucked up*," he muttered, to no-one in particular, closing his eyes again.

They went to sleep in the sun.

ABOUT THE AUTHOR

S.R. Ringuette is a British/French-Canadian crossbreed that successfully reached maturity in the harsh (although friendly) climate of Western Canada. His mission has always been to create entertaining content in some form or another, and has been publishing his cartooning work online since 2007. He is the creator of multiple online web comics: Exploding Wumpus, The Aversion Bureau and Gamer Roommates. In the ephemeral free time he has between meeting cartooning deadlines and preparing for conventions, he has begun to write novels as well. He believes free time is a luxury afforded only to the sane.

Made in the USA
Charleston, SC
11 September 2015